18537

For Joseph, Jennifer, Kerstin, David and Amber
—S.R.M.

To Toni, for keeping it alive
To Shirley, for her patience
To Georgia, our Resshie
—L. & D. D.

Wind Child

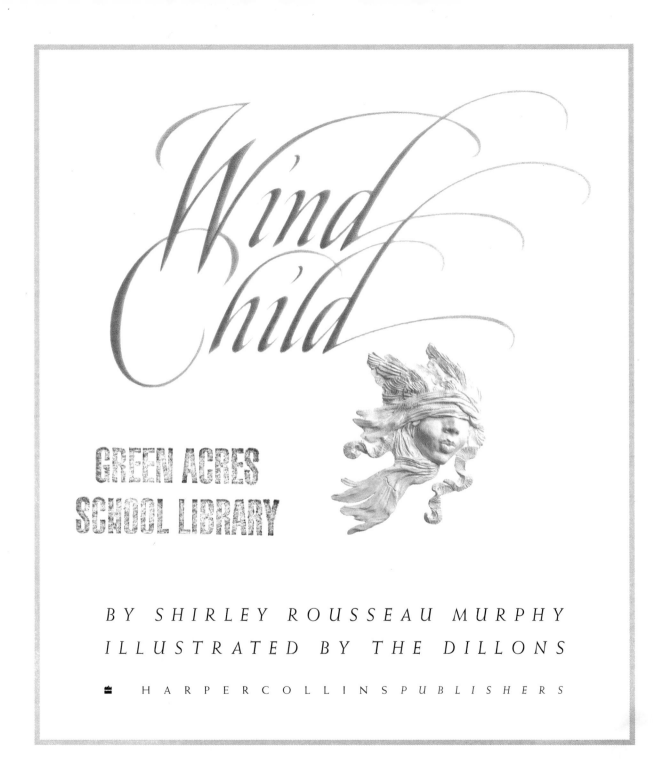

BY SHIRLEY ROUSSEAU MURPHY
ILLUSTRATED BY THE DILLONS

HARPERCOLLINSPUBLISHERS

*O*nce long ago, a stormy wind from the east came into this land, blowing typhoons around him. He was searching for a wife. He found a girl who was not afraid of his wildness. They were wed.

He built her a house of blowing branches and wind-torn cloud. They were happy there. She bore him a daughter, but then she died. The east wind put the baby in the care of an old village woman, and fled back into the sky to be alone with his grief.

He had named the baby Resshie, for the sound his flight makes sweeping through the trees. The little girl grew up wild and dreaming. The old woman never told her who her father was. Resshie wandered the meadows restlessly, watching the winds with a longing she could not understand.

She wanted to know the winds' secrets and what they shouted when they sped across the sky. She yearned to fly as the winds flew, to feel the grasses brush her toes, to leap high above wind-tossed waters.

She tried to send ripples across the water as the wind did, but she was not as skillful. She tried to weave patterns in the rushes like the winds made, but hers were not so beautiful.

Resshie grew into a handsome young woman with pale hair and eyes as changeable as the sky. "Now you are grown," said the old woman who raised her. "Now you must make your own way." And she sent Resshie into the world.

So Resshie took a cottage alone and began to weave rough cloth to earn her bread. But sitting at the loom, she would look up at the blowing winds and wish to weave beauty like theirs.

And I will, thought Resshie. She worked long and hard, until her gauzy cloth seemed made of wind and storm. Soon folk came to buy her weaves, and the village girls wanted Resshie to make their wedding veils. But when Resshie saw how happy the young brides were, she wondered if she wanted a husband too, to share her future.

Soon Resshie's cottage grew too small for all her spindles and dyes and her loom and bolts of cloth. So she wove a new house of willows and grasses, in the windiest patterns she knew—a house so beautiful that passing winds stopped to admire it. She ran to each, holding out her arms and calling. But the winds thought she was a mortal girl and would not speak to her.

There was no one quite like Resshie, to share with her the world's secrets. Few village men would court her; she was too wild, too childlike, too different from mortal girls. And Resshie didn't care for the village men. Those who did come were either too shy or too loud.

Resshie thought, if she wanted a husband, she must weave one.

She wove a man, tall and handsome. She made his body of rushes and rose vines, and his face of heather and wild oat stalks. She wove his hands of fresh corn silk, and his feet of white meadow flowers. When she finished, Resshie whispered wind sounds to him, and the young man came alive.

She called him Summer.

They were happy wandering the meadows. But soon he began to fade. His vines dried out, his flowers withered. He began to sag. At last he fell. Summer was nothing but a pile of bracken that Resshie swept from the door.

So she wove a more durable husband of sheep's wool, the feathers of gulls, and the tough silky tails of horses. She used soft rabbit skin for his cheeks, and wove slivers of horse's hooves into his feet. She dressed him in clothes made from the hides of bulls.

She named him Ormond, which means dragon man, for she thought that would give him strength. Ormond helped her in the garden, and held her warm at night. But Ormond faded, too. His birds' feathers molted. His leathers cracked and fell away.

Soon Ormond also lay in a heap on the floor.

Only then did Resshie understand. Neither Ormond nor Summer had been truly alive; not as the winds are alive, or as a human is.

Now, in the forest wandered a hunter more handsome than the village men. Resshie wove a net of green forest leaves, and carefully she laid her trap, hiding it well. And she caught the hunter.

His name was Clay, which means mortal. Clay thought her beautiful. But he did not want to be captive, and he yearned for his lost, free life.

Resshie saw his sorrow, and she let him go.

Alone again, Resshie worked long hours at her weaves. They grew so beautiful that folk from far countries came to see, and to buy. And all the passing winds swirled around her cottage to look. Resshie called to the winds, longing to go with each across the endless sky. But they did not take her hands or speak to her.

One morning, when Resshie was hanging a length of silk on the bushes, a swift wind circled her cottage. It fingered the silk and made it ripple. It rattled the treetops and pulled at the thatch on her roof. It disappeared only after Resshie had sold the cloth.

The next morning, a rap came on Resshie's door.

A young prince stood there, dressed in silver as glittering as the morning sky. Strange how still the sky was; no wind stirred in it.

"I would like to see the fabrics you weave," said the prince. "They are spoken of across the land."

"And what is said of my work?" Resshie asked.

"It is said to show the heart of the winds. Will you tell me how this can be?"

"Perhaps I understand the winds," said Resshie.

"No mortal can understand the winds," he said, flicking his cape impatiently.

"*I* can," said Resshie.

"Can you prove it?" he challenged.

"I can prove it," Resshie told him. "But if I do, you must promise me one wish."

"How do you know I can grant a wish?"

"Will you promise?" said Resshie stubbornly.

The prince saw a bright wildness about her that he had never seen in a mortal. "I will grant your wish if I can," said he. "What is it, pretty Resshie?"

"I would be your wife," said she, "and travel wherever you travel. In return, I will weave a tapestry that shows *your* true likeness." For Resshie had guessed that he was not a mortal man.

"And if you fail," said the prince, "what forfeit will you pay?"

"I will serve you as handmaiden for all of your days," said Resshie, "always at your bidding."

The prince howled with laughter. Whichever way the wager went, Resshie would win.

At last he nodded, and struck the bargain.

The prince gave her twenty days.

First Resshie dyed her threads crimson and saffron and amethyst, turquoise and cerulean. Then she gathered spiders' webs and wound them on long spindles. She gathered poppies, wild irises, golden hairs from wild horses, and amber rushes from the river. The gathering took five days. When Resshie was finished, she began to weave.

Resshie hardly slept, hardly left the loom. Her tapestry reflected wild skies and the wind-ripples in wheat and the shadows of blowing clouds. Soon the bright cloth spilled over the loom and lay in folds across her cottage.

On the twentieth day, the weave was finished. Resshie lay down on the rug before the hearth and went to sleep. The prince came just at dusk.

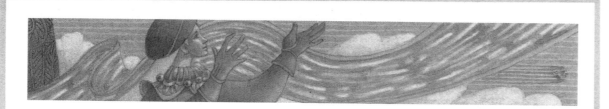

As he approached the door, the thatch on the roof fluttered. He touched the windows, and they trembled. He looked inside and saw Resshie sound asleep. He lifted his hand, and Resshie's bright weaving came to life. It twisted out the door and blew around the prince, then sailed high above the cottage.

Resshie woke and came to see.

The prince took her hand, and together they stood looking. As her tapestry shimmered across the sky, the prince said, "You have, indeed, captured my spirit." And he looked deep into Resshie's eyes.

He said, "You are not a mortal woman." Then the prince did a strange thing. *He* began to weave—but not with thread or straw. He wove with the air itself.

He wove a breeze like silver gossamer around Resshie. As she stood in his windy bower of silver air, the wind-prince put his arms around her.

And so he took her home.

Now from the sky, Resshie and her true love weave the reeds along the world's rivers, and tangle the manes of running horses. They scatter the smoke from a million fires and the petals from roses. They carry birds on silver paths and shake the limbs of trees that thrust up from our world into theirs. Now at last, Resshie is happy.

Wind Child

Text copyright © 1999 by Shirley Rousseau Murphy

Illustrations copyright © 1999 by Leo Dillon and Diane Dillon

Sculpture © 1999 by Lee Dillon

http://www.harperchildrens.com

Library of Congress Cataloging-in-Publication Data

Murphy, Shirley Rousseau.

  Wind child / by Shirley Rousseau Murphy ; illustrated by the Dillons.

    p.   cm.

  Summary: Unaware of her unusual parentage, Resshie grows up
restless and longing to know the secrets of the wind and she uses her extraordinary ability
as a weaver to help her achieve her dream.

   ISBN 0-06-024903-X. — ISBN 0-06-024904-8 (lib. bdg.)

   [1. Fairy tales.   2. Winds—Fiction.   3. Weaving—Fiction.]

I. Dillon, Leo, ill.   II. Dillon, Diane, ill.   III. Title.

PZ8.M957Wi 1999   94-13861

[E]—dc20   CIP

                                           AC

Typography by Al Cetta   1 2 3 4 5 6 7 8 9 10 ❖   First Edition